We show our passports. The passport man looks at me very carefully.
'Enjoy your trip,' he says.

'I hope you haven't any diamonds in there!' jokes a
security officer
'Now please open that tin,' he says to the man
behind me.

He opens the tin and a huge paper snake
jumps out.
'This is my pet,' he laughs. 'I am Marvello the
Magician.'

We wait in the departure lounge and watch for our flight number to appear. Suddenly a lady's voice booms out on the speaker.

'The next flight to...'
I hold my nose. 'I can talk like that, Mummy.'

'Shoosh!' says Mummy. 'That's our flight.'
We walk down a short tunnel. At the end is our
plane.

'Hello. We hope you enjoy your flight,' says an air hostess as we climb in.
'It's my first,' I say proudly.

I am lucky. I have a window seat.
'Fasten your seat belt,' says another air hostess.
'We are about to take off.'

I feel funny. The plane lifts off the ground gently, and in no time we are high up. Below us are tiny little houses.

'You can undo your seat belt now,' says Mummy.
I don't feel funny any longer.

I hear a crackly noise.
'Good day, everyone, this is your Captain
speaking. I'd like to wish you all a good trip.'

I am having a good trip. I am looking at the sea shimmering below.
'Won't you have some lunch,' says the air hostess, giving me a box.

There's chicken, juice and jelly.
I wish I could run through that field of soft, woolly
clouds. 'Can we get out now?'

'I hope not,' laughs Daddy. 'But we are *nearly* there. Oh! Look at the snow on those mountains!'

The mountains gradually turn into hills, as the plane comes down slowly, gently.
Is that cow looking at me?

'Fasten your seat belts, please,' says the air hostess. 'We'll be landing shortly.'

The plane touches down with a slight bump. We've arrived.

The air hostesses are waiting to say goodbye.
'We do hope you enjoyed your first time on a plane.'